You can practica the roasting pe;

Jack followed his grandfather, Bub, from a distance, determined to learn the secret of where he disappeared to every Christmas Eve. So far, the trail led to Glosser Bros. Department Store.

As soon as Jack opened the door of Glosser's, his nose filled with the smell of tobacco and roasting nuts. It was the smell that always came to mind when he thought of Glosser Bros., the rich aroma that permeated his favorite part of the store, the last lobby on Locust Street.

The tobacco counter was on his left, a nook where pipe tobacco, cigars, and cigarettes were sold. Magazine racks lined the wall on his right; two white wire spinner racks stood in front of them, stuffed with bags of coverless comic books.

Moving on, Jack paused at the candy and nut counter, the source of the aroma of roasting peanuts and cashews wafting through the lobby. His mouth watered at the sight of the trays of candy and piles of nuts inside the glass case.

Tearing himself away, Jack ran up the few steps leading out of the lobby. A trio of women nearly knocked him over as he stepped onto the ground floor of the store.

There it was, in all its glory: the heart of the Glosser Bros. department store. The place was a madhouse, packed with people grabbing last-minute gifts...but Bub was nowhere among them.

DEDICATION

To the late, great Bub and Glosser Bros.,
forever alive in my heart.

What happened in the secret sub-basement of Glosser's department store in Johnstown, Pennsylvania every Christmas Eve? Jack Shaffer found out in 1975, when he was eleven years old.

And then he found out what it felt like to die.

*****

"Where did you say you were going?" Mom stared at Jack through slitted eyes, holding one hand over the phone receiver in her grip.

"The library." Jack scrubbed his fingers through his short sandy hair in frustration. Mom had been talking on the phone and hadn't heard him the first two times he'd said it. "There's a book I need to get."

Mom waved him off. "Go on, then." She didn't ask if he was sure the library was open on Christmas Eve, didn't tell him to be careful or hurry home. She wasn't always big on that sort of thing, since her latest boyfriend had moved out.

Jack pulled on his navy blue jacket over his red sweatshirt and bluejeans. "Seeya."

Mom didn't answer. Her hand was already off the receiver.

As Jack zipped up the jacket and marched toward the front door, he heard her talking excitedly into the phone again. "He'll definitely be at church tonight, Deb? You really think he'll like me?"

Scowling, Jack threw the door open and slammed it shut behind him. As he ran off down the street, all thoughts of Mom's dating life shot right out of him. He had bigger things on his mind, a mystery he needed to solve.

One involving the only man he truly cared about in the whole world.

*****

The door on the yellow-sided house two blocks from where Jack lived opened slowly, and a heavy tread came

2

down on the front porch. As Jack watched from behind a tree on the other side of the street, a tall man with wavy silver hair stomped down the four steps from the porch to the sidewalk.

The man wore a dark gray jacket, zipped halfway up over a big pot belly. Under the jacket, he wore the same thing he wore every day--a crisp white button-down shirt and black tie. His trousers were black, too, and so were his immaculately shined Oxford shoes.

If Jack had called out to him at that moment--*Hey, Bub!*--the man would have grinned and waved him right over.   Not only was he Jack's grandfather, Mom's dad, but he was Jack's biggest supporter, always there when he needed him.

Except for one night out of the year, that is. One night when he was nowhere to be found.

Christmas Eve.

Jack waited for Bub to get half a block down the street, then followed, taking care to stay far enough back that he wouldn't likely draw Bub's attention. Whenever he could, he lingered behind trees or lamp posts or parked cars, ever ready to duck down if needed...but Bub never looked back.

He just kept rambling down the street, eyes dead ahead, steering toward his mysterious errand.

Suddenly, a neighbor lady, Mrs. Williams, pushed open

her car door in front of Jack. "Well, hello there, Jackie."
She was in her eighties and stooped with arthritis but got
around fine, even drove herself on errands. "Do you think
you might help me with my groceries?"

Jack shook his head. "I'm sorry, Mrs. Williams, but I
can't. I'm in a hurry."

"But it will just take a minute, Jackie."

"Next time, sorry." Jack's guts jittered when he looked
up ahead where Bub should be. He was nowhere in sight.

Mrs. Williams was saying something, but Jack ran
off without another word. No way was he going to wait
another year to find out Bub's secret.

There was an intersection up ahead, and Jack charged
toward it. Stopping on the corner, he looked right, then
left, then stomped his foot angrily. He saw no sign of Bub
in either direction.

Thinking fast, Jack sprinted forward, hoping for a
glimpse of Bub down one of the cross-streets or alleys. He
didn't spot him at the first street or even the second, but
he caught a glimpse at the third--a flash of Bub's silver hair
and gray jacket sliding past.

Jack gasped in relief and veered right down the side
street. Reaching the end, he leaned out in time to see Bub
disappear around a corner.

"Geez!" Jack panted as he darted after him. The old

man was giving him a run for his money as he navigated the maze of the neighborhood in Dale Borough, not far from downtown Johnstown.

Peeking around the corner, Jack saw Bub continue straight ahead. He fell in behind him, keeping his distance as before.

And wondering what exactly Bub intended to do downtown, since that was where he was headed.

*****

Snow flurries flickered down around Jack as he followed Bub out of Dale. The closer he got to downtown, the more flurries fell, and the colder the wind got.

The skies darkened, too, as afternoon spun toward evening. Plenty of the cars whisking past on Bedford Street had their headlights on, though the streetlights above remained dark.

The snow picked up, and so did Jack's curiosity. Where could Bub be heading on Christmas Eve, alone? Why was he going there?

Every year, he did the same thing, without explanation. Jack always ended up going to midnight mass at St. John's with his grandmother, Gram. As for Mom, she never came along, either, but her travels weren't so mysterious; there was always a new boyfriend in the picture, complete with drama or celebration or both.

Bub left the bigger gap, as far as Jack was concerned. He'd been Jack's father figure and best friend for the past seven years, for most of Jack's life. Not having Bub around cast a shadow on Christmas Eve; he was always back for Christmas Day, but it was never enough.

And every year, the mystery of his whereabouts haunted Jack a little more. It had become one of the overriding mysteries of his life, right up there with *Why did my Dad leave when I was four years old and is he ever coming back?*

Now, as Jack got closer to an answer, his heart beat faster. He was on the verge of discovery, he could feel it; nothing would be the same after that.

Bub ambled across Haynes Street and kept going, making a beeline into town. He glanced in the front window of the Bedford Street Newsstand, waved at someone inside, but didn't slow down.

When Jack reached the newsstand, he looked in and saw an old-timer looking back at him, scrawny and shriveled in a pale blue polyester leisure suit. The old man eyed him as he passed, giving a little half-nod before returning his attention to the magazine rack.

By the time Jack looked forward again, Bub was two blocks ahead, rounding the corner of Main Street. No question, he was making good time; for a man with a big pot belly, he could really move when he wanted to.

Imagining he was Colonel Steve Austin, the bionic hero from his favorite TV show, *The Six Million Dollar Man*, Jack broke into a full-tilt run. Arms and legs pumping, he blasted across Vine Street--getting honked at by a car about to make a left turn--and covered the remaining distance to Main in nothing flat.

Worried that he might have lost Bub, he eased around the corner for a look down Main...and felt a wave of relief. Bub had stopped a block away, across from the McDonald's restaurant, and was talking to an old woman dressed in red. Her hat, coat, dress, and shoes were all red; maybe she was going to a holiday function...but if so, where was the green to go with the red?

As Jack watched, Bub reached out and put a hand on her shoulder. Had this been his goal from the start? Meeting up with a secret girlfriend?

But then, with a few more words, he let go of her and continued on his way down Main Street. Meeting the woman wasn't his last stop after all.

Jack still thought there was something funny about her, though. As he walked past her on his way to follow Bub, he took a good look...and felt a shiver up his spine. Her eyes, when he gazed into them, were misaligned, each looking off to either side instead of straight ahead. Jack couldn't tell if she was looking right at him or not.

He was all too happy to get past her, especially as Bub was already turning another corner. He was a block ahead on the other side of Main, zipping right on Franklin Street.

Channeling the Six Million Dollar Man, Jack bolted after him. As he ran, he heard the sound effect from the TV show in his head, the sound like high-tech motors and parts cranking and straining in artificial legs: *ch-ch-ch-ch-cha, ch-ch-ch-ch-cha.*

The latest course change brought him to the heart of the action, the middle of town. Central Park, on the left, was filled with little cottages, each decorated with Christmas paraphernalia. The trees in the park were all decorated, too; just as Jack rounded the corner, every one of them lit up at once, hundreds of bulbs glowing blue, red, yellow, and green amid the falling flurries.

The park and the sidewalks around it were busy with people, most of them hurrying with arms full of shopping bags. The bags were all stamped with a familiar logo, a name printed with a flourish on the brown-and-white-striped paper. It showed where they'd been...and where Bub was now headed. Whether it would be his last destination remained to be seen, but Jack knew it was where he was going right now.

Glosser Bros. The big department store facing the park, on the corner of Franklin and Locust.

Bub was crossing Locust, marching toward Glosser Bros. department store...for what reason, Jack still didn't know.

*****

As Jack hung back, staying on the park side of Locust, Bub ambled up to the door on the corner. Another old-timer was standing there, spindly as a scarecrow in a black-and-white houndstooth sport coat, bright green Alpine hat with a big white feather in it, and brown-and-red plaid pants.

Grinning, the old-timer shook Bub's hand with gusto. Jack couldn't hear a word they said, but they rattled on like old buddies for a while.

Then, the old-timer hugged Bub and shuffled into the store with a jaunty wave. Bub didn't follow him in, to Jack's surprise; instead, he walked down Locust Street along the side of the dark brick building, weaving between the knots of last-minute shoppers and people gazing at the window displays.

That was Jack's cue. Darting across Locust, he threaded through the crowd in Bub's wake.

But he didn't make it past the windows as fast as Bub did. They were one of his favorite Christmas traditions; every year, Glosser's employees decorated them to the hilt, filling them with holiday scenes centered around mechanical figures.

Jack had already seen this year's editions, but he couldn't help stealing glances again. There was one with Santa checking names off a giant list with an orange quill pen while elves built toys around him. In another, a drummer in a tall black hat and red uniform beat a drum in front of a Christmas tree dripping with white lights and tinsel. Another window was done up like an undersea kingdom with a blue backdrop; Santa, wearing scuba gear, rode a sleigh pulled by dolphins, surrounded by branches of coral draped with glittering lights.

Jack didn't consider himself a little kid anymore, but he still loved those windows. They brought back memories of years gone by, gazing through that same glass with Bub and Gram...or, further back, with Dad. Sometimes, he felt like he could just reach right through and touch them, if the moment was right and no one was looking. Or maybe he could just ask Dad a question, get him to lip-read if he couldn't hear the sound...then Jack could lip-read his answer in return. He'd looked for that moment, looked for Dad's reflection more than a few times.

Just as he now looked away from the windows for the answer to the Christmas Eve mystery. Up ahead, he saw Bub hang a sharp right, entering the store through the last door on Locust Street.

Pacing himself, Jack took his time getting to that door. He didn't know exactly where Bub was going and didn't want to get caught following too closely.

When he got to the door, he cupped his hands around his eyes and peered through the glass. Bub was nowhere to be seen.

As soon as Jack opened the door, his nose filled with the smell of tobacco and roasting nuts. It was the smell that always came to mind when he thought of Glosser Bros., the rich aroma that permeated his favorite part of the store, the last lobby on Locust Street.

The tobacco counter was on his left, a nook where pipe tobacco, cigars, and cigarettes were sold. Magazine racks lined the wall on his right; two white wire spinner racks stood in front of them, stuffed with bags of comic books. Jack had gotten comics there for as long as he could remember, three to a bag; sometimes, he picked them out himself, and other times, Bub brought them home as a treat. None of the comics had covers, which was why they were sold so cheap, but Jack loved them just the same.

It looked like the racks were freshly stocked, and Jack

had to force himself to look away. Moving on, he paused at the candy and nut counter, the source of the aroma of roasting peanuts and cashews wafting through the lobby. His mouth watered at the sight of the trays of candy and piles of nuts behind the glass case.

Tearing himself away, Jack ran up the few short steps leading out of the lobby. A bustling trio of women loaded with packages nearly knocked him over as he stepped out into the spacious ground floor of the store.

There it was, in all its glory: the heart of the Glosser Bros. department store. To the left of where Jack was standing, shoppers jostled among displays of shoes and boots, shouting and waving for the attention of overwhelmed salespeople. Straight ahead, in the big middle section, people crowded around tables overflowing with merchandise--everything from hats and gloves to shirts and socks. On the far side of the store, shoppers swarmed racks of menswear and coats, inspecting items from top to bottom and trying them on, then slinging them over forearms or tossing them aside.

The place was a madhouse, packed with people grabbing last-minute gifts...but Bub was nowhere among them. Jack saw plenty of familiar faces in the crowd under the glittering decorations, heard the chorus of voices mingling with the Christmas music piped in over the intercom system...but neither saw nor heard a trace of his grandfather.

Bub was in there somewhere, though. He had to be, unless he'd ducked out another door. If he wasn't on the ground floor, he must be on another level of the store.

Jack darted left, weaving through the mob like a football player navigating downfield. Cutting off a fat lady with a baby in each arm and a shopping bag hanging from each hand, he hopped on the escalator heading up.

*****

When the moving stairs reached the second floor, Jack jumped off. Women's clothing and lingerie occupied most of level two; maybe Bub was looking for a last minute present for Gram.

Giving up on caution, Jack sprinted all around the second floor. He snaked between the clothing racks and tables, craning his neck for a glimpse of Bub's telltale silver hair. Every step of the way, he ducked shoppers casting glares in his direction, especially when he cut them off or bumped into them.

By the time he'd finished his circuit of the women's department, he was out of breath...but maybe not out of luck. Grimly determined, he bolted down the short hallway into the Annex, an adjacent building connected to the main body of the store.

The second floor of the Annex seemed like a better choice than the women's department...not because it was home to the notions department with all its sewing supplies, but because it was also home to Glosser's Cafeteria.

As Jack passed through Notions, a sales clerk frowned at him--an old woman he'd seen there often, who'd worked there for ages. As always, her lipstick extended beyond the middle section of her upper lip, forming a double arch of deep red that reached up under her nose.

Jack ignored the dirty look she gave him and continued on to the cafeteria. He knew the place well; he'd been there many times with Bub over the years. It was one of their favorite places to eat, right up there with Stuver's Crispy Chicken and the Bradford Room in Grant's Department Store in Richland, a Johnstown suburb.

Bub wasn't anywhere in sight today, though. The airy, brightly lit dining area was full, but Bub wasn't sitting there. He wasn't in the cafeteria line, either, or standing at the ice cream counter.

Jack hurried over there anyway. As he approached the counter, the twins who worked there--who'd worked there as long as he could remember--both gave him a bright smile.

"What would you like?" The two women said it at the same time, with identical high-pitched voices.

"Uh, hi." Jack had never been able to tell them apart; they were both short, with deep brown eyes and black hair pulled back in a bun. They wore matching uniforms, too--pink and white striped aprons over white dresses with short, puffy sleeves. "Have you seen my grandfather here today? He's tall, with white hair, and..."

"Of *course* we know your grandfather," said one of the twins.

"Rocky Road in a waffle cone is his favorite," said the other twin. "He's always in here."

"But not today," said the first twin. "Sorry."

Jack slumped. "Thanks anyway."

"So sorry." The second twin patted the side of the freezer beside her. "Would you like a sample on the house?"

Jack glanced over his shoulder, feeling jumpy. His only goal was finding Bub and solving the mystery.

But when one of the twins handed him a flat wooden spoon topped with a clump of chocolate hard-packed ice cream, he didn't turn it away.

He licked the spoon clean in a heartbeat, then dropped it in the little trash can beside the counter. "Thanks!"

"And what else?" Both twins asked the question at the

15

same time.

Jack couldn't help grinning. "Nothing, thanks." Turning, he hurried back toward the elevators. "Merry Christmas!" He shouted it to them as an afterthought.

In reply, the twins started singing Christmas songs--one, "White Christmas," the other, "Santa Claus Is Coming to Town." Their high, piping voices sounded strange singing different things at the same time instead of speaking in unison.

*****

Jack sprinted back down the hallway into the main building, running a serpentine course through overloaded shoppers. Charging straight for the elevators, he punched the button with the arrow pointing up. Since the escalator only reached the second floor, this was the quickest way to the upper levels.

The bell dinged, and the door closest to Jack slid open on a full car. Jack squeezed in anyway, hearing shopping bags crumple as people shifted to make room. At least he didn't have to reach across for the buttons; the one labeled with the number 3 was already lit.

When the door opened again, Jack popped out of the crowded car onto the third floor. Just as he started searching the housewares department, a woman's voice spoke over the storewide intercom system, interrupting the holiday music.

"Glosser's will close in fifteen minutes," she said. "Thank you for shopping at Glosser's, and have a very Merry Christmas."

So now the clock was ticking. If Jack didn't find Bub soon, he would have to end the search and get out of the building.

Adrenaline sizzling in his bloodstream, Jack hurtled among the blankets and pillows, the curtains and cookware and blenders and sweepers. Moving on, he barreled through the furniture department, hoping for a glimpse of Bub on a sofa or rocker/recliner.

But he came up short again. That left the fourth floor, Jack's next favorite place after the candy and comics lobby.

When an elevator didn't come right away, he went for the stairs. He took them two at a time, climbing fast to the store's top floor, where they kept the good stuff.

The toys. Bursting through the door, Jack found himself facing a mother lode of them...a Fort Knox of playthings, a Scrooge McDuck vault overflowing with every cool toy his heart desired. Right there on an endcap display--*right there*--was the fabled Colonel Steve Austin, the Six Million Dollar Man doll, twelve inches tall, complete with a plastic silver engine block for Steve to toss around like a feather and a rocket capsule to reenact the accident that led to him becoming bionic. Jack wanted that doll so bad he could taste it, wanted it more than anything for Christmas '75.

Except for the answer to the mystery of where Bub went on Christmas Eve, that is.

Snapping back to the mission at hand, Jack dashed through the toy department, looking right and left...seeing nothing but toys and late shoppers.

Skidding to a halt by the elevators, Jack punched the only button there, a down button. There was only one more place where he might find Bub, assuming Bub hadn't left the store or backtracked to one of the floors Jack had already searched.

This time, when the elevator door opened, the car was empty. Jack leaped inside and hammered the bottom button on the control panel, the one with a big letter "B" printed on it.

He was going all the way down now, all the way to the bargain basement.

*****

As soon as the elevator door opened at the last stop, the woman's voice came over the intercom again.

"Glosser's will close in five minutes," she said. "Thank you for shopping at Glosser's, and have a very Merry Christmas."

Jack's heart pounded faster than ever now, as time kept running out. Frantically, he scanned the basement...though he wasn't feeling hopeful. It was starting to look like Bub would get to keep his secret another year after all.

Though, truthfully, Jack couldn't say that for sure at first. The basement was a madhouse as always; the crowd down there was thicker than anywhere else in the store.

Men, women, and children--mostly women--swarmed the rows of tables lining the space under bright fluorescent lights. The mob of shoppers tussled over heaps of merchandise, everything from purses to underwear to razors, all of it deeply discounted.

The bargain hunters didn't seem to be slowing down, either. If anything, the five-minute warning seemed to have ratcheted up their frenzy. People bumped and elbowed each other to grab the best junk from the piles. The hubbub they made was loud enough to drown out the piped-in Christmas music.

Careful not to get hit by a deal-crazed grandma, Jack worked his way across the room, checking one face after another. Some were familiar, but none belonged to Bub.

By the time Jack crossed back to where he'd started, he

felt the crush of impending defeat. He started thinking of other places he could look, places other than Glosser's; Bub must have given him the slip and gone elsewhere.

Maybe he was at a bar with his old buddies from Bethlehem Steel, where he'd worked for 40 years. He'd retired from Bethlehem five years ago, but he still liked drinking with the guys whenever he got the chance.

Or maybe he was playing cards at the retired men's club, where he also liked to hang out. Or maybe he'd gone to a movie at the Embassy or State theaters on Main Street. Anything was possible.

Then, suddenly, it wasn't.

Jack made one last trip across the basement and turned to work his way to the exit. At that instant, his eyes grazed past the crowd to the far wall...just in time to catch sight of an open elevator there.

Jack's eyes widened. He couldn't believe what he was seeing. Bub was right there in the elevator, calmly staring into space.

Heart racing, Jack started forward. He'd only taken three steps when the elevator door slid shut, and Bub disappeared from view.

But at least he wasn't far. At least Jack finally knew where he was and had a chance to catch up.

Breathless, he ran the rest of the way across the

20

basement to the elevator. He glanced up at the arrow light beside the closed door. The arrow pointed upward, as always; it should have been lit to indicate the car was heading to an upper floor.

Except it wasn't.

Jack frowned. There was only one direction to go from the basement, and that was up. Bub had to be heading for an upper level. Therefore, the light must be broken.

Jack flicked his eyes to the indicator bar above the elevator door, the one that showed what floor the car was on according to what number was illuminated. He expected to see the number 1, 2, 3, or 4 lit up, indicating that Bub had stopped on one of those upper floors. Instead, he saw something he'd never seen before, something he couldn't explain.

For a split-second, Jack saw the letter "X" appear and light up to the left of the numbers. He blinked hard, then looked again, and it was still there.

X.

Then it was gone, and all the numbers on the indicator bar were dark.

*****

"Glosser's is now closing," said the woman's voice over the intercom. "Thank you for shopping at Glosser's, and have a very Merry Christmas."

As shoppers hurried out of the bargain basement with their merchandise, Jack slumped in the corner, moping. His secret mission was over; the store was closing, and he had to leave.

The chase across town had been for nothing. Jack would have to go another Christmas without solving the mystery.

He hated the thought of giving up and going home. He knew his failure would hang over him all through Christmas Eve and Christmas Day. Even a 12-inch Colonel Steve Austin the Six Million Dollar Man doll under the tree wouldn't make him feel better...not all the way better.

Because Jack would still have to wonder, as he did every year, if Bub was sneaking off to see someone important. Someone who might want to keep tabs on the family once a year at least...especially on Jack.

After all, Bub and Jack's dad had always gotten along really well, hadn't they? Even though Mom was Bub's own daughter, and Dad had skipped out on her, Bub had never seemed to hate him, had he?

Jack knew it was probably a childish pipe dream--he'd always known it in his heart--but still, he'd held on to his hope. He'd imagined, if he followed Bub on Christmas Eve, that Bub might lead him to Dad in the flesh. And maybe, in the spirit of the season, they might settle some things between them.

But now, that childish dream was melting away like ice between his fingers. He had to let go of it, at least for another year.

Pushing away from the corner, Jack stuffed his hands in the pockets of his jacket and started for the steps leading out of the basement. The rest of the crowd and employees had already climbed up out of there, leaving Jack as the last straggler.

Or was he?

Just as he was about to put his foot on the bottom step, he heard two familiar, high-pitched voices chirping in unison behind him. "We can send you to him, if you like."

Whirling, Jack saw the twins from the ice cream counter standing five feet away, smiling at him. Each of them held a waffle cone of double-scooped Rocky Road hard-packed ice cream.

Jack looked around and frowned. "Where did you come from? I didn't see..."

"The Annex, silly." The twin on the right laughed. "Here." She pushed her cone of Rocky Road in his direction.

Jack took it, feeling creeped out. He hadn't seen or heard a trace of the twins until they got his attention. "No, I meant..."

"Right this way, please." Both twins said it at once as they turned and started walking. "We will send you to him."

Jack followed...though deep inside, a warning bell was going off like crazy. He'd known the twins forever--known them to buy ice cream from them, anyway--but something didn't seem right about what was happening. "What do you mean, 'send?'"

The twins led him across the room to a silver aluminum Christmas tree in the far corner. A device on the floor cast light on the tree from a bulb behind a slowly turning color wheel. The tree turned red, then yellow, then blue, then green...then red again.

"The ice cream will help you pass the time," said one of the twins.

Jack's frown deepened. "What do you mean, 'pass the time?' How much time am I going to have to pass?"

Without answering, the twin who'd given Jack ice cream bent down and picked up the color wheel device. Walking away from the tree, she aimed the device under one of the bargain tables, casting colored light into the shadows.

As the wheel kept turning, the cement floor under the table changed from yellow to blue to green. When it turned red, a rectangular outline appeared, five feet long by three feet wide...only to disappear when the color returned to yellow.

"What the heck?" Jack bent down for a closer look, but the rectangle was gone. He couldn't see the faintest trace of it, at least when the light was yellow, blue, or green.

But when the red beam shone again, it came back. And this time, Jack saw more detail than before. In the middle of the edge closest to him, there was an indentation--four inches long, cut into the substance of the rectangle.

Jack's ice cream was dripping, but he didn't notice. "What *is* this?"

"Something you must swear never to breathe a word of to anyone," said the twin with the color wheel.

"If you make it back," said the other twin.

"*If?* What do you *mean*, *if?*" asked Jack.

"Do you swear it?" asked both twins at once.

Jack knew he was in over his head. This craziness was like something out of a movie or TV show...like something Colonel Steve Austin might face. It was exciting, but a whole lot scarier than he'd ever imagined an adventure could be.

"Do you swear it?" repeated the twins.

"Will I find my grandfather if I don't?" asked Jack.

The twins smiled and shook their heads.

"Then fine," said Jack. "I swear it."

"Hold this, please." The twin who still had an ice cream cone handed it over.

Jack took it, leaving him holding two cones...one of which was dripping. Raising the dripping cone, he took a half-hearted lick around the rim, stopping the worst of the leak...then suddenly couldn't care less if every bit of both cones melted at once.

Because one twin was opening a door that shouldn't have existed. Crouching alongside the table, she reached down, touching her fingertips to the floor. When the color wheel turned red again, the indentation reappeared, less than an inch from her hand. She pushed her fingers into it and pulled up with a loud grunt.

And the rectangle of floor lifted up, revealing a hole. A doorway.

"There you go." The twin stopped pulling when the slab of floor was canted at a 45-degree angle. It couldn't go any higher unless someone moved the table out of the way.

"Now hurry," said the other twin, taking one of the ice cream cones back from Jack. "Move it or lose it." She looked over her shoulder as if expecting trouble.

"I don't know." Jack swallowed hard. "You're sure he's down there?"

Both twins raised their eyebrows. "Have we ever

served you bad ice cream?" they asked.

"Well, no." Jack shook his head.

"And we're not serving it to you now," said the twins. "Everything you want to know is through there." They pointed at the doorway in the floor.

Suddenly, the woman's voice spoke over the intercom again. "Glosser's is now closed. All associates, please escort any remaining guests out of the store."

"Time's up," said the twin with the ice cream. "Close it."

As the other twin took hold of the door, Jack's heart pounded. What if this was his last chance to find out where Bub had gone? "Wait!"

"No time," said the twin at the door.

Footsteps clacked in the distance; someone was coming down the stairs...an associate, maybe, looking for stray shoppers.

"Here!" Jack gave his cone to the twin who didn't have one. Dropping to his knees, he scooted under the table to the edge of the hole. Looking down, he saw dimly lit spiral stairs winding around a shaft walled with gray stone blocks. "Where do I go?"

"All the way down," said the twins. "To the bottom."

Jack had a split second of indecision...then slid his feet over the edge. He dangled them into the shaft, stretching to reach the first step with his toes, and lowered himself down.

Ducking, he eased down a second step, then a third and a fourth. By the time he got to the sixth, the top of his head was just above floor level in the bargain basement.

"Don't forget your ice cream." The twin Jack had given his cone to handed it down to him. "Use it to pass the time."

Jack didn't really want it, but he took it anyway. "Thanks. Thanks for everything."

"Good luck!" said the twins.

Then, as Jack continued downward, they shut the door after him. When he looked up, he couldn't see a trace of it.

*****

Jack shivered as he descended the spiral stairs...as much because of the cold as because he was scared of what he might find at the bottom. A chilly draft swirled up from below, moaning in the passageway and cutting right through his clothes. He wished he'd put on a heavier coat when he'd left the house on Bub's trail.

Needless to say, he wasn't really in the mood for ice cream anymore. He still held on to the cone, though, because there wasn't a good place to leave it. He thought better of putting it down behind him, just in case he had to get back up those narrow stairs in a hurry.

Not that he was in a hurry going down. The stone steps were worn smooth, as if lots of people had walked them in the past. It wouldn't take much to slip and fall, especially in the dim, flickering light.

Jack thought it looked like torchlight on TV or in the movies, dancing up through the stairwell from below. It didn't amount to much near the top but got a little brighter as he descended. Even so, it left deep shadows along the inner wall and played tricks with his eyes. Several times, he thought he saw something moving in the gloom, slithering beyond the next bend...only to realize it was just the flickering glow.

Or was it?

The whole time Jack walked deeper underground, every hair on the back of his neck stayed standing at attention. Ever since the twins had revealed the door in the basement floor, he'd had the feeling he was moving into uncharted territory, a twilight zone in which anything might be possible. He half-expected to see Rod Serling himself appear around the next turn.

Jack had always loved shows like *Twilight Zone*, had watched them religiously. It had been so much better to dive into fantasy and science fiction than deal with the problems of his own broken family and crappy life. But being in the middle of a creepy scenario himself didn't seem like quite as much fun as watching one on TV. In spite of the twins' assurances about what awaited him downstairs, he couldn't help dreading the outcome.

But he had to keep moving anyway. He couldn't turn back, the door was gone...and he needed to see for himself if Bub was at the bottom.

The question was, how far down did Jack have to go to get there? The stairs just kept leading him deeper and deeper; he wasn't counting, but he knew he'd already gone down lots more than it should have taken to get from one basement to another. There were so many, he needed a break after a while and stopped to sit down for a moment. He even had a lick of the ice cream, which wasn't melting as fast in the cold.

Continuing onward, Jack wondered when it would end. Had the twins led him into some kind of bizarre supernatural trap? What if he spent all eternity just walking down those steps, trying to get somewhere that didn't exist?

When he took a second break, though, he heard something...some kind of sounds in the distance. Was it just his imagination, or was he hearing faint voices wafting up from down below?

As Jack resumed his descent, he moved slower than

before, listening intently. Just as the flickering light kept brightening the further down he went, so did the sounds get louder.

A few more steps, and he could tell for sure: they were voices, all right. He didn't know what they were saying, but he could tell they were human voices.

Heart pounding, Jack continued to creep toward them. He realized his long trip down was almost over, though he still had no idea if that would be a good thing. Whatever Bub was mixed up in, it was unusual, to say the least. If Jack's ominous descent down that dim, dank stairway was any indication, it might be dangerous, as well.

As Jack got closer, the voices got louder, until he could finally distinguish between them. There were three: an old man's voice, high and gravelly; a woman's, deeper and throatier; and a younger man's, deeper and louder than the rest.

"What do you want us to say?" asked the woman. "Times are changing."

"New times, new terms," said the old man. "You understand."

"It's nothing personal," said the younger man. "Just business."

Suddenly, a fourth voice spoke. "It's *personal*, all right." This voice, Jack knew by heart. "It's nothing *but* personal."

Bub. It was *Bub.* The twins had not steered Jack wrong, after all.

But what were Bub and the others talking about? Jack had to get closer to find out.

"It's a *negotiation*, Ben," said a fifth voice, that of another old man. "Same as it is *every* year."

"You're not negotiating," said Bub. "You're doing the *opposite*. You're not giving me a leg to stand on."

"Did you think you could keep doing this *forever*?" asked the woman. "Postponing the inevitable one year at a time?"

"Yes," said Bub. "Now tell me what I need to do to make this deal. Tell me what you want from me to make it worth your while."

"Honestly?" The first old man, the one with the high-pitched voice, cackled. "You're wasting your *breath*. We want *nothing* from you anymore.

"This town is doomed to *die*, and there's nothing you can do to save it."

*****

Finally, Jack reached the end of the shaft. As he walked off the bottom step onto a floor of dusty cobblestones, the old man's last words echoed in his mind.

This town is doomed to die, and there's nothing you can do to save it.

Jack wondered what it meant. What had he stumbled into here?

And how exactly was Bub involved? What had the woman meant when she'd said he'd been "postponing the inevitable, one year at a time?"

No doubt about it, Jack needed to get closer. He needed to hear more, to understand what was happening.

Taking care not to make a sound, Jack tiptoed toward the voices. He saw an entryway in the gray stone wall ahead, a gap through which the flickering light was flowing, and he headed straight for it.

There was a curved rim along the base of the gap, a crescent-shaped lip with a large stone in the middle. Breathing fast, Jack stepped over it, watching carefully to make sure he didn't trip and fall.

But when he got both feet on the other side and looked up, he almost fell over anyway. He felt instantly dizzy and light-headed when he took in the scene around him; it was a miracle he managed to stay upright.

Because somehow, everything and everyone but him was upside-down.

Jack stood at the edge of a large chamber hewn of the same gray block as the stairway. The voices that had drawn him there were coming from the middle of that chamber, and the people they belonged to were upside-down, seated or standing on the ceiling. The circular table and chairs they occupied were upside-down, too.

So were the blazing torches and the framed paintings and photos on the walls. So was the statue of the big red dog across the room--Morley's dog, a legendary canine from the 1889 flood.

Everything had been flipped...or, maybe, it was all perfectly *normal*. Looking back at the entrance he'd come through, Jack suddenly thought of an explanation for the curved lip along the bottom. What if that was the *top* of an *archway* instead of some kind of inexplicable low ledge?

But what Jack was thinking couldn't be true, could it? Wasn't it impossible to defy the law of gravity like that?

Apparently not. As Jack stood there, trying to adjust to the off-kilter scene, a stream of ice cream melted from his cone...and ran straight *up*. It dribbled past his head and kept on going, running toward what seemed to be the ceiling from his point of view.

Except it was the floor. And Jack was the only occupant of the room who was truly upside-down.

*****

Jack hastily licked at the ice cream cone to keep any more from falling. Somehow, doing that made him feel less dizzy and light-headed, as if something in the ice cream was a cure for vertigo.

Meanwhile, the group at the table up above (down below?) kept talking. Luckily, the room was an echo chamber; the people were in the middle of the room, at least thirty feet away, but their voices carried so well that they sounded like they were right next to him.

"There must be *something* you want," said Bub. "There always is." He was standing in the open well in the middle of the circular table. His jacket was gone; his bright white button-down shirt took on a reddish glow in the torchlight.

"Not this time," said the old man with the high-pitched, gravelly voice. Now that Jack had a clear view of him, he could see he was the old-timer Bub had waved at in the Bedford Street Newsstand, the one in the pale blue polyester leisure suit.

Jack recognized two others at the table, also: the old lady in red whom Bub had spoken to on Main Street and the old man in the houndstooth sport coat and brown-and-red plaid pants whom Bub had hugged in front of Glosser's.

"Events have been set in motion," said the lady in red. "Events that have been too long delayed already."

"The death of Johnstown, Rachel?" Bub shook his head angrily. "That can *never* be delayed too long."

"Now, now." The old man in houndstooth fiddled nervously with his green Alpine hat on the table in front of him. "It will only be temporary, Ben."

Suddenly, the younger man spoke, the one with the deepest, loudest voice. "Damn right!" When he jumped to his feet, Jack could see he was tall and broad-shouldered, rippling with muscles like a body-builder. "You can't keep Johnstown down! It'll be *back*, baby, bigger and better than ever!"

"You tell 'im, Steel Toe!" The man in the powder blue leisure suit clapped his hands.

"Which is, of course, the whole point, isn't it?" said the man in houndstooth.

"The cycle of death and rebirth," said Rachel. "There can be no true progress without it."

"At a cost of how many lives?" asked Bub.

"A drop in the bucket, Benny." Powder blue leisure suit leaned back in his chair and hoisted his feet on the table. "*Less* than a drop. A *drip*."

"Those people out there are your *charges*." Bub gestured up at the ceiling, which was also Jack's floor. "Isn't that what you've *told* me?"

"I'm Mr. Flood!" Powder blue leisure suit pumped

his gnarled fists in the air. "*My* only charges are the storm clouds and lightning bolts!"

"No, it's true," said houndstooth. "We're like parents to them...and as such, we know what is *best* for them."

"Which is *death*?" Bub threw his arms open wide. "For how many, Joe? Hundreds? Thousands?"

Houndstooth--Joe--shrugged and looked away. "I can't say."

"Whatever it *takes*," snapped the muscle man.

"Whatever the flood waters can carry." Mr. Flood's feet jiggled around in their white buck shoes as if the idea tickled him.

For a long moment, no one spoke. Above them, Jack watched in amazement, trying to sort out what he'd heard.

Who *were* these people? Were they actually talking about flooding Johnstown? Could they *do* it?

And how had Bub come to try to talk them out of it? Was this really what he did every Christmas Eve?

Jack shivered. There he was, in a scenario worthy of the Six Million Dollar Man, and he just wanted to get out of it. He just wanted to get back to his boring, crappy life again and forget about life-or-death deals in sinister hidden lairs.

He was starting to think he would've been better off not knowing Bub's secret after all.

*****

Rachel was the one who finally broke the silence. "You need to accept reality, Ben. The covenants are yesterday's news."

"I wouldn't say that." Bub turned in her direction. "We've negotiated them every year since I was, what... twenty-five? And my father did the same before me."

"You *had* to bring *him* up, didn't you?" Mr. Flood swung his legs off the table and lunged halfway out of his chair. "That sweet-talking son of a gun!" He stood all the way up and wriggled his hands in front of his chest effeminately. "'Ohh, that terrible flood in 1889!'" he said in a falsetto, mocking voice. "'Johnstown can't stand another disaster like that! Please, can't we make a bargain to keep this town safe?'"

"It was a *hard* bargain," said Bub. "You've only ever agreed to a year at a time."

"Poor baby!" shouted Mr. Flood. "Do you have any *clue* how *lucky* you were to get even *that*?"

"What about '36?" said Bub.

"Ah, '36." A broad grin stretched across Mr. Flood's cadaverous face. "A good year. A *very* good year."

"So that's what *this* is?" said Bub. "1936 all over again?

Tear up the covenant, flood the city, get your jollies?"

"Why the hell not?" Mr. Flood slammed his palms down on the table. "You've been holding this town back for too long, Benny! How do you expect this place to *grow up* if we keep *babying* it?"

Bub leaned in and locked eyes with him. "You don't need to kill thousands of people for this town to grow up."

"You're spoiled!" Mr. Flood sneered. "You've been getting what you want for too long. Well, the gravy train stops *here*, my old not-friend."

Bub leaned closer. He had an expression of fury on his face that Jack had seen only a handful of times in his life. "You twisted, miserable..."

"Hey!" Steel Toe jumped up and threw down a fist between Bub and Mr. Flood. "Back off, Ben! I don't *care* if you're a *union man*, I'll smack you *down* if you lay a hand on him!"

For a moment, Bub stayed right where he was, glaring at Mr. Flood. "*You* don't want progress. *You* don't want this town to grow up." He leaned a little closer then, making Steel Toe tense up. "You might have fooled the others, but you haven't fooled *me*."

"Says the biggest fool in the room." Mr. Flood howled at his joke and threw himself down in his chair.

"That's enough!" shouted Joe. "There will be no

further conflict here." He picked up his green Alpine hat and plunked it on his head. "This matter is settled."

"You must accept what has been ordained." Rachel looked around the table grimly with her misaligned eyes. "The next great flood will strike Johnstown next year, in July of 1976."

"Just in time for America's Bicentennial." Mr. Flood let out a little whoop. "Talk about fireworks!"

"Consider yourself fortunate, Ben," said Joe. "You've been given enough warning to move your loved ones elsewhere."

Bub backed away from Mr. Flood and slumped. "Please." He held out his hands to Joe and Rachel. "Please, no. All those people..."

"Will be a tragic loss," said Rachel. "And none of us takes joy in that."

Mr. Flood cleared his throat loudly.

Rachel ignored him. "But it doesn't change the fact of what is coming. We all must accept and look beyond it to the new and stronger Johnstown that will rise up in the wake of this disaster."

"Till the next one." Mr. Flood snickered.

"No, wait," said Bub. "There must be something we can do. There must be something I can give you."

Just then, at that exact instant, a blob of Rocky Road

ice cream hit the floor at the edge of the room with an echoing splat.

*****

Jack had forgotten about the ice cream. He'd been too caught up in the conversation to remember to keep licking it.

The melting had slowed in the cold underground chamber but never stopped completely. Eventually, the Rocky Road had turned to mush and dropped right out of the cone.

So now, his secret surveillance was at an end. All eyes in the room were locked on him.

"Jack, no!" shouted Bub.

"Again with the drama?" Mr. Flood scowled like a rotting peach. "Would someone please get that brat out of here?"

"Jack, run!" Bub waved frantically, trying to shoo him from the room. "As fast as you can!"

"No need to be inhospitable," said Joe. "This is your grandson?"

"Aren't you going to introduce us?" asked Rachel.

Bub wouldn't take his eyes off Jack. He jerked his head, signaling him once more to leave.

But Jack was frozen where he stood. He knew he should do what Bub told him and run--he *wanted* to get away--but he felt pinned down by the pressure of all those eyes upon him.

"Well?" said Rachel.

"This is Jack," said Bub. "Let him go. He isn't a part of this."

"That remains to be seen," said Rachel. "How long have you been standing there, Jack?"

Still gaping at Jack, Bub drew his thumb and index finger across his lips as if he were pulling a zipper across them. The message was clear.

Jack kept his mouth shut.

"How much have you heard?" asked Joe.

Bub shook his head. Jack got the clear impression it wouldn't be good for him to say anything.

So why did he feel such a powerful compulsion to speak? Why did he have to fight so hard to keep himself from answering the question?

"Shy child." Rachel smiled. "Perhaps we should finish the introductions first. Ben, will you do the honors?"

Bub flicked his eyes hard to the side, another signal. But when Jack didn't run, he sighed and spoke. "Jack, this is Rachel Adams."

"I'm kind of a local legend," said Rachel. "You've

heard of Rachel Hill?"

Jack nodded. Of course he knew about Rachel Adams, everyone did. She was a settler...in the 1700s.

Killed by Indians.

"This is Joseph Johns," said Bub, gesturing at the man they'd been calling Joe.

"Yes, *the* Joseph Johns." Joe laughed. "Founder of Johnstown. *Late* founder, as far as most people know."

Jack swallowed hard. He'd guessed there was magic at work here, some kind of supernatural forces...but *dead people*?

"This is Steel Toe." Bub gestured at the man with the superhero build.

"Spirit of the steel mills," said Steel Toe, grinning and waving. "Any grandson of a steelworker is okay in my book."

"And this..." Bub gestured at Mr. Flood.

"Is your worst nightmare!" Mr. Flood lunged up and hissed loudly, baring his teeth.

"We're all local legends, Jack," said Rachel. "We have an *influence* around here, and we use it for the greater good of Johnstown."

"Your grandfather here has been a...consultant of ours for some time now," said Joe.

"More of an advocate," said Rachel, "for certain local

interests."

"Until he done got *fired*," said Mr. Flood.

"There are men like him all over the world," said Rachel. "Pleading their case with people like us. Keeping it all from falling apart for one more year."

"So, Jack," said Joe. "Is there anything you'd like to ask us?"

Bub's eyes widened, and he shook his head once.

Jack remained silent at first. He knew he shouldn't say anything that might get him in any deeper than he already was.

But then, suddenly, he wanted to talk. As scared as he was, a mob of questions pressed to be let out. This might be his only chance to get answers.

Shaking and sweating and breathing fast, Jack opened his mouth and spoke. "Can you really do it? Flood Johnstown, I mean?"

"Can we *do* it?" Mr. Flood smacked the table with both hands. "How'd you like a lungful of *water*, you disrespectful *guttersnipe*?"

"Hey!" Bub whirled around to glare at Flood.

"Enough!" snapped Joe. "Both of you!"

"The answer to your question is yes, Jack," said Rachel. "We can indeed make such a thing happen."

Jack thought it over for a moment...and another

question came to mind. This time, he directed it at Bub. "What did you give them?"

Bub frowned, looking puzzled. "What do you mean?"

"Every year, when you made the deal," said Jack. "The one to hold off the flood. You said they wanted something to make it worth their while."

Bub started to say something, but the others cut him off.

"He gave us his youth," said Joe. "And his energy."

"He gave us his *dreams*," said Rachel. "His dreams to be anything other than a shop steward in a steel mill in the town where he was born."

"He stayed *here*." Joe tapped the table with a bony finger. "He put Johnstown first."

"It's called *sacrifice*, boy." Mr. Flood sneered. "Giving up something *important*, something you want more than *anything*. It's what you're *supposed* to do, to keep people like us happy."

"But you're not happy now?" Jack pointed at Bub. "You don't want what he has anymore?"

"*Now* you're catching on," said Mr. Flood. "Grampa's all used up. He's circling the drain."

Jack fell silent. As crazy as the situation was, he thought he understood it.

A great flood would strike Johnstown in 1976, killing

hundreds or thousands of people. Bub, who'd always managed to put it off before, couldn't stop it this time. It looked as if no one else could...but maybe it was just that no one else had tried.

An idea was forming in Jack's mind. He knew Bub wouldn't like it; Jack didn't like it much himself. But Jack and Bub weren't the ones who mattered, were they?

The thousands of people in the path of the flood were the ones who mattered.

"Well, Jack?" asked Joe. "Have we answered your questions?"

"Why don't you come down from there and have a proper visit then?" said Rachel.

"I've got some crazy *mill stories* you're gonna love," said Steel Toe.

The longer Jack considered his idea, the more frightening it became...and the more *real*. He trembled at the thought of it, shivered fiercely from the inside out.

"Come on down, Jack," said Joe. "Just walk down the wall."

"But don't knock off any of the pictures, of course," said Rachel.

Mr. Flood chortled. "Unless you'd rather *we* come up *after* you?"

Jack opened his mouth to speak, then closed it. He

knew he was about to make a huge mistake.

But he also knew one other thing. When he asked himself what Colonel Steve Austin, the Six Million Dollar Man, would do in this situation, he only came up with one answer.

Anything he could.

"Wait." The word sprang out of Jack before he could call it back in. "What about me?"

"What *about* you, you ugly little urchin?" asked Mr. Flood.

Jack's voice shook. The enormity of what he was doing left him quaking in his sneakers. "What if *I* sacrificed something?"

For a moment, the room was dead silent. All eyes were glued to Jack again...though only Bub's were wide with horror.

Finally, Joe spoke up. "What do you have in mind?"

*****

Jack swallowed hard. "What if I stay here like Bub did? What if I put Johnstown first like you said?"

"That's a nice thought, dear," said Rachel. "But didn't you hear what we said about events being set in motion?"

"This has already been decided," said Joe. "We've

47

made up our minds."

"No, wait." Jack's mind raced. "What about my youth and energy? I've got plenty of both."

"Jack, stop," blurted Bub. "You don't know what you're saying!"

"Doesn't matter." Joe adjusted his Alpine hat. "The cycle of death and rebirth must continue."

"We've put it off long enough," agreed Rachel.

"You heard the lady." Mr. Flood hiked a thumb in her direction. "Take your youth and energy and stick 'em where the sun don't shine."

Jack felt like he was losing ground fast...but like Colonel Steve Austin, he had to do everything in his power to save innocent lives. "*Dreams*." The word shot out of him like a cannonball.

"Jack, no!" shouted Bub.

"I'll give you my *dreams*, too," said Jack.

"They're *using* you," said Bub. "They'll take *everything*, if you let them!"

"Why don't you put a sock in it?" snapped Mr. Flood. "You're dead wrong, anyway. There's nothing he or *anyone* could offer to delay this glorious flood!"

"Actually...," said Joe. "Let's not be hasty."

"*What?*" Mr. Flood's eyes bugged out of his knobby skull.

"I'm just saying." Joe shrugged. "Now that I think about it, an infusion of new dreams and vitality might not be such a *bad* thing, would it?"

"Yes!" said Mr. Flood. "If it means putting off the flood of the century *again*, then yes it *would* be."

"You might be onto something, Joe," said Rachel.

Mr. Flood leaped out of his chair. "You're not actually *considering* this, are you?"

"What else could you give us, Jack?" asked Rachel. "*If* our minds weren't already made up, that is."

"Nothing!" said Bub. "Don't listen to him! He's just a child!"

"I can't believe I actually agree with *Benny* about something," said Mr. Flood. "Don't listen to that kid!"

Joe ignored him. "What else could you offer us, Jack? What else could you offer for a new covenant?"

Jack thought hard, trying to block out Bub and Mr. Flood, who were both yelling. What could he, an eleven-year-old kid, possibly have to offer to save hundreds or thousands of lives?

He could think of nothing on the same scale, nothing that might be worth trading for all those lives. But then he remembered what Mr. Flood had said about sacrifice...how it had to be something important, something you wanted more than anything.

"The 12-inch Six Million Dollar Man doll," said Jack. "With rocket capsule and engine block." Even as he said it, he hated the thought of doing without it. "I asked for it for Christmas this year."

"And you want it that badly, Jack?" asked Joe. "It means that much to you?"

Jack nodded emphatically. "Oh, yeah." He didn't have to exaggerate his sincerity at all. "It means everything." That toy was at the top of his Christmas list; it had dominated his dreams and daydreams for months, ever since he'd first seen it in the Sears Christmas catalogue.

"Hmm." Joe looked at Rachel. "What do you think?"

Rachel shrugged. "We already agreed not to postpone the flood any longer."

"Damn skippy!" hollered Mr. Flood. "'76 is set in stone!"

"On the other hand," said Rachel, "I suppose I'm not averse to spicing things up." She turned her misaligned eyes on Joe. "What about that wild card we talked about?"

"Hollywood." Joe nodded. "The hockey movie."

"I loved that idea!" Steel Toe pounded the table and grinned. "Lots of opportunities for union work!"

"A new local legend," said Rachel. "One that ripples around the world and far into the future. Some will call it one of the greatest sports movies of all time."

"Yes!" Steel Toe slammed the table again.

"No!" wailed Mr. Flood.

"But the patterns are clear," said Rachel. "It can only happen in 1976. If there's a flood, there will be no *Slapshot*, or any of the movies that come after."

Joe stared into space with eyes narrowed. "It's a different approach, that's for sure."

"A *stupid* approach!" said Mr. Flood.

"But surprises can jump-start evolution," said Rachel. "And this movie will certainly be a great surprise."

"You want a surprise?" snapped Mr. Flood. "How 'bout a couple million gallons of water roaring through town at once?"

Joe ran a finger back and forth along the brim of his Alpine hat. "I don't like changing course once a decision has been made..."

"You tell 'em!" said Mr. Flood.

"But in this case, it might be worth exploring the permutations." Joe smiled up at Jack. "The deal you've proposed has merit."

"No, please," said Bub. "He's a child, he doesn't know..."

Joe looked around at the other occupants of the table. "All in favor of making this deal?"

Everyone but Mr. Flood and Bub raised their right

51

hands.

"Wait!" shouted Bub. "*Stop!*"

All eyes turned to him.

Bub's shoulders heaved, and his face was flushed with stress. For a moment, he said nothing, just stared up at Jack.

"If you insist on doing this, I suppose I can't stop you," said Bub. "But you need to know something." He looked down at the people around the table. "He needs to know something."

Joe made a sweeping gesture with one arm, giving him permission to continue.

Bub looked back up at Jack. "Before you sign anything, you can ask for something else. Something for *yourself*, Jack, to sweeten the deal."

"I can?" said Jack.

"But you don't *have* to," said Joe. "Isn't another year's reprieve from a devastating flood enough for you?"

"*No*," snapped Bub. "Jack, no. Listen to me. Ask for something else. You won't get another chance."

Jack thought about it. "Anything? I can ask for anything?"

"What do you have in mind, child?" asked Rachel.

"Put off the flood longer," said Jack. "How about that? Make it *ten* or *five* years instead of *one*."

"Never!" howled Mr. Flood. "If it were up to *me*, you wouldn't even get *five minutes*!"

"Sorry, but no," said Joe. "The contract is for one year. That's non-negotiable."

Jack looked at Bub, who shrugged and nodded. "Can I *warn* people, at least? Tell them to move away before it hits?"

"Warn whomever you like," said Rachel. "They won't believe you without some kind of proof."

"Jack," said Bub. "You're a good boy, wanting to buy more time and save people's lives...but you need to ask for something for *yourself*."

Jack frowned.

"You're paying a steep price for this deal," said Bub. "Much steeper than you know." He nodded gravely. "Isn't there something you've always wished for? Something that could make up for all the things you're giving away?"

"I don't know." Jack shook his head. "I don't know what to say."

"There must be *something*," said Bub. "Something that could make your life better in spite of the burden you're taking on."

Jack wracked his brain...and then he found it. "Wait... yes." He came up with the one thing he wanted more than the Colonel Steve Austin doll. "I know what I want."

When he said it out loud, he knew it was right. It was perfect. It was what he'd *always* wanted most in his deepest heart of hearts.

And everyone at the table, except Mr. Flood, agreed to it.

"It's a deal." Smiling, Joe plucked the white feather from his Alpine hat. "Now just hold still a moment, young man."

"Why?" Jack asked with a frown.

"Our covenant can only be sealed one way." Joe held up the feather, quill first, and pitched it at Jack like a paper airplane. The feather spiraled its way up to him in lazy loops, white tufts fluttering along its length. "In *blood.*"

Jack's eyes widened. Before he could back away or defend himself, the feather suddenly shot toward him. The tip of its quill punctured his left thumb, shocking him with a pinprick of pain...then popped free and zipped back down to Joe.

"Very good." Joe reached up and snagged the feather from the air, then turned to Rachel. "Contract, please?"

Rachel snapped her fingers, and a parchment scroll appeared on the table between them. "Sign here." She unrolled the scroll and pointed to a line on the bottom with a big black "X" beside it.

Joe positioned the bloody feather above the line, then

let go of it. The feather stayed hovering in place, its bloody tip just above the start of the line. "Jack? Pretend you're signing your name, won't you? The feather will do the rest."

Hesitantly, Jack raised his right hand, pinching his thumb and forefinger together as if he were holding a pen. Then, he scribbled an imaginary signature in thin air.

Glancing down below, he saw the feather scratch across the scroll in exactly the same way, leaving a bright red scrawl on the line beside the "X."

"Done." Joe grabbed the feather, pricked his own left thumb, and signed on the line below Jack's name. "And done."

Rachel waved her right hand in a circle, leaving a trail of glittering sparks that hung in midair. "Now this next part might feel a little uncomfortable."

"What next part?" asked Jack.

"Tough it out, li'l guy!" said Steel Toe. "It'll be over before you know it!"

"But what part are you talking about?" asked Jack.

"When you make a deal with us, you're reborn," said Rachel. "But you can't be reborn if you don't die first." With that, she leaned forward and blew out a big gust of breath.

It sent the sparks flashing toward Jack, expanding as

they went. By the time they reached him, they'd become a cloud big enough to engulf him...which they did.

Instantly, Jack's feet left the floor. As he floated upward in the grip of the glittering cloud--or downward, from the point of view of those around the table--he became paralyzed. No matter how hard he tried, he couldn't move a muscle.

Drifting further, Jack felt his body stiffen and go cold. His breathing stopped, and so did his heart.

Am I dying? As the thought came to him, Jack saw a fresh burst of sparks which might have been in his head. Then, a curtain of blackness fell over his vision, and he couldn't see outside himself anymore.

A rush of memories rushed up to take the place of Jack's darkened sight. He remembered the first time he'd gone to a Pirates baseball game at Forbes Field in Pittsburgh. He remembered the first time he'd gone camping in a tent at Prince Gallitzin State Park. He remembered getting his tonsils out and eating Rocky Road ice cream in his hospital bed while watching cartoons.

With his father. In every one of the memories that came to him, his father was there.

He was part of lots more, too...so many moments that Jack hadn't thought about in ages. Going grocery shopping at the supermarket; skinning a knee on a gravel driveway;

sitting in church on a Sunday morning; crying on a shoulder over something unimportant. Dad was there every time, his face and voice and presence woven through the fabric of Jack's life in ways Jack had forgotten.

Then Dad was gone, too, and so were those moments. And so was Jack.

He had a distant awareness of touching down, settling onto the floor that had been his ceiling. Then that, too, faded, as did his awareness of himself.

All was dark and silent and still, a vacuum. Nothing remained of Jack or anything he knew or thought or wanted, not even the faintest impression of an absence in the void, like a wisp of perfume left behind in a room.

*****

The first thing Jack saw when he opened his eyes was the giant Christmas tree decoration on the corner of the Glosser Bros. building. It was made up of V-shaped rows of white lights, broad at the bottom and narrower further up. An eight-pointed star perched atop the peak, glowing softly in the falling snow.

Watching that tree, which had towered over Christmas for as long as Jack could remember, he felt completely at peace. He didn't have a single worry, didn't have a single need.

He smelled the icy air of a winter's night, felt snowflakes gently falling on his face. His body bobbed up and down, carried away from Glosser's glowing tree in someone's strong and steady arms.

The only thing he heard was the soft buzz of Glosser's lights and the labored breathing of whoever was carrying him. Turning his head, he looked up and saw a familiar face staring straight ahead--eyes squinting against the snow, cheeks and forehead flushed and glistening with sweat, silver hair fluttering in the wind.

"Bub?" Jack's voice was a squeak.

Bub looked down at him, his smile as warm as the air was cold. "Welcome back, Jack." A familiar parchment scroll brushed his cheek; the scroll was sticking up from his shirt pocket under his jacket, rolled up and tied with a shiny red ribbon.

Seeing that scroll started bringing back Jack's memories of what had happened in the secret chamber under Glosser's. "I'm...alive?"

Bub nodded. "Alive and kicking, Fauntleroy." It was a nickname he sometimes used for Jack. "On your way home in time for Santy Claus to come."

Jack heard church bells in the distance and frowned. He felt exhausted, as if he might drift off at any moment.

"Bub?"

"Yes, Jack?"

"Did it really happen?"

Bub's expression turned grim. "You shouldn't have followed me, Jack. You shouldn't have been there."

Jack yawned loudly. "But did it really happen?"

Bub didn't say anything for a long moment. He kept his eyes focused ahead, blinking away snowflakes.

"Yes, Jack." Bub nodded toward the rolled-up scroll in his pocket. "The contract with your signature on it is right there."

"Huh." Jack's eyes fluttered shut. He wanted to stay awake but couldn't seem to make it happen. "I could've sworn it was all a crazy dream."

"No, Jack." Bub's voice sounded sad as well as strained from carrying his grandson. "I'm sorry to say it wasn't a dream at all."

*****

Jack woke the next morning to the sound of "Step Into Christmas" by Elton John playing on his clock radio. Though he'd slept like a rock through the night, he was still so exhausted that he let the song play through to the end.

When he finally managed to reach over and switch

it off, he dropped right back into a deep sleep. His experiences of the night before had left him so drained, he couldn't even drag himself out of bed on Christmas morning.

A knock on the door nearly woke him up again, but Jack ignored it. He was lost in a dream about Penn Traffic, the other department store in downtown Johnstown; Colonel Steve Austin was there playing Santa, fighting reindeer terrorists with laser-emitting noses.

But then the knock at the door repeated, followed by a voice. "Jack?" It was Bub. "Jack, can I come in?"

Jack groaned and rolled over on his side, wishing Bub would leave him alone. He wasn't ready to deal with human contact yet, not until he'd slept a while longer and sorted out his bizarre memories from last night.

But Bub wasn't ready to give up. "Jack?" He knocked louder. "Are you okay in there?"

Jack flopped on his back and scowled at the ceiling. The room was awash in bright white light, the kind that flares around the edges of the curtains on a snowy morning. He guessed it was after ten even before he looked over at the numbers displayed on the face of his clock radio: *10:15*.

There was a long pause until the next knock. "I'm coming in, Jack."

The doorknob turned slowly, and the bolt clicked free of the jamb. Jack wished he'd locked it the night before... but the truth was, he didn't even remember getting home. He had a vague recollection of gazing up at Glosser's Christmas lights and being carried in Bub's arms; then nothing.

Had Bub carried him all the way home and put him in bed? It would explain why Jack was still fully dressed under the blankets, wearing the same red sweatshirt and bluejeans he'd worn to Glosser's. Only his navy blue jacket had been removed.

"Are you all right?" Bub opened the door halfway and peered in with a look of concern.

Jack nodded. "Just tired."

"Good, good." Bub eased in the rest of the way and shut the door behind him. As always, he was wearing a white button-down shirt, black tie, black trousers, and black Oxfords. "What you went through last night..." He lowered his voice. "It can be pretty rough on you."

"Tell me about it," said Jack.

Just then, the radio popped back on, blasting "Santa Claus Is Comin' To Town" by Bruce Springsteen. With a loud grunt, Jack smacked the off switch on top of the device, silencing the music.

"You look okay otherwise, though," said Bub. "That's

a good sign."

"I guess so," said Jack.

Bub looked uncomfortable. "If you ever want to talk, let me know." He paced to the window at the foot of Jack's bed and tugged back the edge of the curtain, peeking outside. "I've been through it all at this point. I can answer your questions."

Jack sat up and swung his legs off the edge of the bed. Now that he was awake, certain questions did come to mind. "How will they take them?" he asked. "The things I said I'd sacrifice?"

"A little at a time." Bub sighed. "You won't even notice they're gone...for a while, at least."

"But I promised to give them my youth, my energy, and my dreams. How can I *not* notice they're gone?"

"I misspoke." Bub turned from the window and narrowed his eyes. "What you'll notice...the way you'll give those things up...is by never leaving this town. Then your youth and your energy will fade over time as they always do."

"I'll never leave town?" said Jack.

"You'll never *want* to leave," said Bub. "One day you'll wake up, and you'll be sixty-five years old...and you'll realize you're still here. You'll just end up stuck here."

"Stuck here?" Jack had never thought much about the

future, had never thought about leaving or where he might want to live someday. But thinking about it now gave him a funny feeling in the pit of his stomach.

"It won't be so bad, Jack," said Bub. "Johnstown's a good place. A *decent* place. It's worth saving. It's worth *staying*."

Jack frowned. "But the deal's only for one year. I can leave after that, can't I?"

Bub shrugged. "Why would you, if there's still a chance you can save everyone? A chance you can buy another year?"

"I could do that?"

"Why not?" Bub's eyes twinkled. "My first contract was only for a year, too."

Seeing the look on his grandfather's face made Jack smile. Maybe things would work out okay after all. Maybe it wouldn't be so bad following in the footsteps of Bub, and Bub's father before him. There were huge responsibilities and a price to be paid, but it might all be worth it in the end. After all, saving lives was its own reward, wasn't it? Wouldn't Colonel Steve Austin be proud?

And there was another reward, too, that Jack had forgotten until now. "What about that thing I asked for? The one to sweeten the deal?"

Bub peeked outside again. "What about it?"

"You don't think they'll go back on their word, do you?"

Bub snorted and let the curtain fall back into place. "Not a chance." He headed for the door. "Steel Toe won't let them take away a good union man's fringe benefits."

Just as he said it, the doorbell rang.

Bub opened the bedroom door. "C'mere a minute, Fauntleroy. There's something you should see." He nodded for Jack to follow and stepped out into the hallway.

As the two of them walked downstairs, the doorbell rang again. No one else was running to get it; Jack guessed Mom was at her boyfriend's place.

Turning a corner at the bottom of the stairs, Jack stole a glance at the Christmas tree in the living room. Even from a distance, he could see that the telltale red-and-white box of the Six Million Dollar Man 12-inch doll wasn't among the few gifts scattered under the tree. Jack spotted books and clothes and a basketball, but no Six Million Dollar Man. So the local legends had held him to the terms he'd agreed to; Jack had said he'd sacrifice that toy--which had been at the top of his list, so he'd been sure he was going to get it--and they'd taken him up on the offer.

But that was okay. Jack was willing to give it up, if it meant saving Johnstown.

And anyway, he wasn't even thinking about it thirty

seconds later. It was the furthest thing from his mind when Bub opened the door, and Jack saw who was standing there.

"Hi, Jack." The man at the door was a little older than Jack remembered. His dark brown hair was frosted with gray, and his eyes crinkled when he smiled. "Merry Christmas."

Jack was dumbstruck. He stood there staring at the man on the front stoop, not knowing what to say or do next.

His heart was racing like Colonel Steve Austin chasing down a speeding motorcycle. His eyes were locked on the man's face, zooming in and scanning every detail as if they were bionic.

"So how are you?" asked Bub as he shook the man's hand. "What brings you back to these parts?"

"Actually..." The man shrugged and shuffled his feet, uncertain. Then, he straightened and smiled. "I'm moving back to town."

"Is that so?" Bub looked at Jack. "How do you like that?"

Jack was still tongue-tied. He'd gotten what he'd asked for in the chamber under Glosser's, and he'd gotten it right away...like magic. This was exactly what he'd asked for to sweeten the deal, the one thing he'd wanted more than anything in the depths of his beating heart.

"I've been thinking," said the man, nodding as snowflakes fell gently around him. "Maybe I could see you once in a while, Jack. If you'll let me."

Jack just kept staring.

"Maybe we could talk a little first," said the man. "I could explain a few things. Clear the decks, so to speak."

"What do you say, Jack?" asked Bub.

Jack had been brave enough to face down Joseph Johns, Rachel Adams, Steel Toe, and Mr. Flood in the mystery basement under Glosser's, but he still held back from talking to this one ordinary man. There was so much history between them, so much hurt, so much loss. And now, there was a chance to start over, and Jack wanted it more than he'd ever wanted anything in his life.

But seeing the man in front of him was so much different than daydreaming about it. The pressure of reality made it all so much sharper and more dangerous.

"Well, Jack?" said the man. "Do you have time to talk?"

It was Christmas Morning, and a potentially wonderful gift had landed on Jack's doorstep. The question now was, what should he do about it?

Exactly what Colonel Steve Austin would do.

"Sure, Dad." Jack stuck out his hand. When Dad shook it, he felt an electrical tingle run up his arm, like the power surge in a bionic limb performing a superhuman feat. "I'm not going anywhere, am I?"

ABOUT THE AUTHOR

Robert Jeschonek is an award-winning writer whose fiction, comics, essays, articles, and podcasts have been published around the world. DC Comics, Simon & Schuster, and DAW have published his work. His young adult slipstream fantasy novel, *My Favorite Band Does Not Exist*, won the Forward National Literature Award and was named a Top Ten First Novel for Youth by *Booklist*. His cross-genre science fiction thriller, *Day 9*, is an International Book Award winner. He also won the Scribe Award for Best Original Novel from the International Association of Media Tie-in Writers for his alternate history, *Tannhäuser: Rising Sun, Falling Shadows*. He was nominated for the British Fantasy Award for his story, "Fear of Rain." Visit him online at www.robertjeschonek.com. You can also find him on Facebook and follow him as @TheFictioneer on Twitter.

ANOTHER GREAT JOHNSTOWN STORY NOW AVAILABLE FROM ROBERT JESCHONEK

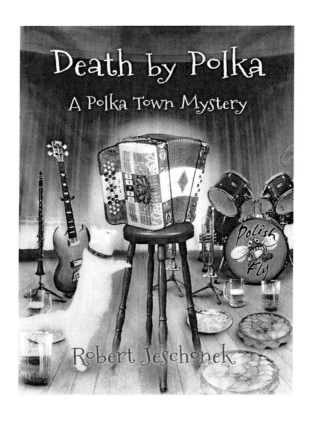

DEATH
BY
POLKA

BY ROBERT JESCHONEK

Who killed Polish Lou, the famous Prince of Polka Music? His daughter, musicologist Lottie Kachowski, comes home to the polka heartland of Johnstown, Pennsylvania, to find the answer. Lottie has an unbeatable talent for using music to solve crimes, and she does just that on the trail of her father's killer. But the stakes turn deadlier than ever when another polka legend comes to a tragic end. As the danger rises, Lottie recruits her father's wacky girlfriend, Polish Peg, to help her dig deeper into the wild world of small town polka. At the same time, she fights to keep from getting dragged back into the polka scene she left behind long ago.

AND NOW, A SPECIAL PREVIEW OF
DEATH BY POLKA...

As I looked out over the crowd in the banquet hall, the Furies glared back at me in disgust. There were three of them, all dressed in black, all with raven black hair, and they were my sisters.

Bonnie, the oldest and tallest, stood in the middle. Her brown eyes framed a big, angular nose that gave her the look of a hawk. Her hair was long, draped over her shoulders, but not nearly as long as mine.

Charlie stood at her side. She was shorter and rounder than any of us, with plump cheeks and dark blue eyes. Her hair was cut in a kind of dowdy helmet 'do that made her look older than she was, older than any of us.

Then there was Ellie, the youngest. She looked like an anorexic teen, all skin and bones and giant blue eyes so pale they were almost white. Those eyes peering out from

1

her shag haircut with the spiky bangs looked perpetually challenging, always ready to go off.

Which, actually, described her personality. All *three* of the Furies' personalities.

Boy did they have capital "T" tempers. They were always, *always* fighting with each other, shifting alliances, holding grudges on top of grudges.

But today, for once, they were united against a common object of resentment. *Me*, in other words. I had the honor of having brought them together in harmony. I could see it in their body language as they all clustered together and stared up at me through slitted eyes. I could feel it in the air, and I could guess what had brought it on.

They were mad that I was the only sister called up on stage. It didn't matter that I didn't *want* to be there; I knew my sisters, and I *knew* this was eating them alive.

It was just the latest in a series of injustices. First, I'd gone off to Los Angeles while they'd all stayed in town and given birth to the ADHD Dozen. Then, I'd gotten engaged, while the best they'd been able to manage was a string of deadbeat baby daddies. Now this.

I knew I'd pay for it later, but I chose to ignore them for now. Basil Sloveski was waving a number ten white business envelope over his giant silver pompadour.

"All right, folks!" The corners of Basil's eyes crinkled as

2

he grinned. Up close, I could see his whole overtanned face was a web of fine lines. "Without further ado!"

The crowd roared (except for the Furies, who just rolled their eyes) and pumped beers in the air. The ADHD Dozen squirmed their way up front and lined up along the stage, screeching and dancing like idiots.

"How about a drum roll, guys?" When Basil said it, Eddie Sr.'s ancient drummer hopped up on the stage, raised his bony arms in a weight-lifter's pose with fists curled toward his shaggy white head, and dropped down on the squeaky red stool behind his drum kit.

As the drum roll started, Basil slid a fingernail under the corner of the envelope flap, then dragged his nail along the length of the flap, tearing it open with a ripping sound.

My heart pounded, and I held my breath. As badly as I didn't want to be there, I was actually caught up in the suspense. Polish Lou's showmanship had broken through even my tough exterior.

The kids down in front couldn't stand the suspense either. They were hopping up and down, clawing at the stage, having conniptions. Milly spoke for all of them. "*What? What's it say?*"

Basil slipped two tanned fingers into the envelope and drew out a folded sheet of paper. He cleared his throat as he unfolded it, playing up the drama.

Then, he started reading. "Dear fellow polka lovers!" The drum roll continued in the background as Basil's voice rang over the crowd. "As you know, I've been called the Prince of Pennsylvania Polka."

The crowd roared its approval.

"But now that the *Prince* is dead, who will rule his *kingdom*?" Basil paused and looked around the banquet hall for dramatic effect. "Who will be my *successor*?"

"*Who? Who?*" squeaked one of the kids down in front.

"Who will carry on the tradition of great polka music as leader of my band, Polish Fly?" read Basil. "Who will continue to broadcast three hours of polkatacular tunetasticness every Saturday morning and Sunday afternoon on my radio show, *Kocham Taniec*?

"Who will organize the annual Polkapourri festival that has become an institution for Johnstown and the entire tri-state area?

"And who will manage Polish Lou Enterprises now that Polish Lou is gone?" Basil stopped reading aloud, though his eyes kept scanning the page. He got a funny look on his face, a kind of smirking frown, like he wasn't sure he'd read the letter correctly. Then he shrugged, nodded, and gazed out at the crowd. "I'll tell you who!

"*She* will!" With that, Basil swung an arm around and pointed directly at Peg.

The drum roll ended with a rim shot, and the crowd cheered like crazy. Eddie Sr. and Eddie Jr. played wild strains on their accordions. In front of the stage, the kids spun and jumped and gyrated like human popcorn in their little suits and dresses.

Glancing at the Furies, I saw the three of them looked more thoroughly disgusted than ever. One thing they all had in common and shared with me was an undying hatred of Polish Peg.

As for the Clown herself, she beamed and waved with pure delight. If I hadn't known any better, I might've thought she'd just won the Miss America pageant or an Academy Award.

Clapping politely, I turned away and looked for the best place to step down from the stage. The crowd was slightly thinner by the corner, so maybe that would be a good exit point.

Just as I took a step toward the corner, Basil called out behind me. "And *she* will, too!"

I swear, everyone in the banquet hall gasped at once. Except me.

"That's right!" said Basil. "I'm talking about *you*, Lottie!"

At the mention of my name, I spun to face him. "Me, what?"

"You're the *co-queen* of Lou's kingdom, that's what!"

Basil lunged over and grabbed my arm, then hauled it high like I'd just won a prize fight. "Ladies and polkamen! Meet the new rulers of Polka Land! Lou's own daughter, Lottie..." Basil grabbed Peg's arm and hefted it overhead alongside mine. "...and his partner, the love of his life, Polish Peg!"

The crowd went berserk. Cameras flashed in my eyes as Eddie Sr. and Eddie Jr. launched into "Hail to the Chief" on their accordions.

Dazed, I leaned forward and looked past Basil at Peg. The look on her clownish face said it all.

She was as surprised as I was. And just about as happy.

Which, let me tell you, wasn't happy at all.

Pie Press

CPSIA information can be obtained at www.ICGtesting.com
Printed in the USA
LVOW12s1303151213

365394LV00001B/292/P